A Kid is a Kid is a Kid

written by
Sara O'Leary

illustrated by
Qin Leng

(g)

GROUNDWOOD BOOKS
HOUSE OF ANANSI PRESS
TORONTO / BERKELEY

BEING the new kid is hard.

I can think of better things to
ask than if I'm a boy or a girl.

"What a question!"

"I get asked why I always have
my nose in a book."

"Books are my life!"

"I get asked why
I'm so small."

"I'd rather get asked what big words I can spell."

"I get asked where I come from. Here. I come from here."

"I don't know why we are always asked
if we're identical twins!"

"I was asked why I didn't have any friends."

"Then this boy said,
'I'm their friend.' And
now he is."

"Asking me why I wear the same shirt all the time isn't logical."

"I mean, just look. It's an exceptional shirt."

"Why would anyone ask me why
my sister was born different?"

"Everyone's different."

"Ask me what I can do,
not what I can't!"

"Ask me my new dog's name."

"Pumpkin Pie!"

"Ask me if you can try my lunch."

cabbage
(kimchi)

rice rolls

shrimp
pancakes

tofu soup

"I love to share."

dumplings

"I wish you would ask me about my grandmother's house."

"I was so happy there."

"You know,
there's one question
we all like."

"Hey, kid! Do you want to play?"

For Graham McDonald, my kid brother. — S.O'L.

•

For my little kid, Lou, and for all kids! — Q.L.

Published in 2021 by Groundwood Books / House of Anansi Press
groundwoodbooks.com

Groundwood Books respectfully acknowledges that the land on which we operate is
the Traditional Territory of many Nations, including the Anishinabeg, the Wendat
and the Haudenosaunee. It is also the Treaty Lands of the Mississaugas of the Credit.

We gratefully acknowledge for their financial support of our
publishing program the Canada Council for the Arts,
the Ontario Arts Council and the Government of Canada.

With the participation of the Government of Canada
Avec la participation du gouvernement du Canada | Canadä

Library and Archives Canada Cataloguing in Publication
Title: A kid is a kid is a kid / written by Sara O'Leary ; illustrated by Qin Leng.
Names: O'Leary, Sara, author. | Leng, Qin, illustrator.
Identifiers: Canadiana (print) 20200394347 | Canadiana (ebook) 20200394363
| ISBN 9781773062501 (hardcover) | ISBN 9781773062518 (EPUB) | ISBN
9781773065922 (Kindle)
Classification: LCC PS8579.L293 K53 2021 | DDC jC813/.54—dc23

The illustrations were done in ink, watercolor and pastel.
Design by Michael Solomon and Lucia Kim
Printed and bound in Canada